Where Do I Sleep?

A Pacific Northwest Lullaby

Jennifer Blomgren

Illustrated by Andrea Gabriel

SASQUATCH BOOKS
SEATTLE

Where do I sleep? Just offshore in a bay,
I rest on the surface and dive when I play.
Look out for my mother and me when you sail;
We're gentle and mild. I'm a baby Gray Whale.

Where do I sleep? On a pillow of grass—
I nap on the tundra as long hours pass.
The sun in the summertime always stays up
In Alaska, my home; I'm a Gray Wolf pup.

Where do I sleep? In a den snug and warm—
While winter storms blow, it's here that I'm born.
When spring comes I'll go and look for some grub—
Fresh leaves and bugs! I'm a Brown Bear cub.

Where do I sleep ? On an island cliffside—
In a nest under rocks I quietly hide.
You might see me fly near the seashore in spring.
I'm a baby Horned Puffin, called a Puffling.

Where do I sleep? At the edge of the tide,
Beneath the green waves where the seabirds ride.
Watch out where you wade, so you don't step on me
In my tidal pool home; I'm an Anemone.

Where do I sleep? In a drifting kelp bed—
I lie on mom's belly, the stars overhead.
Lulled by the rise and the fall of the water
Close to the shore, I'm a baby Sea Otter.

Where do I sleep? Overlooking the Sound,
In a big nest of sticks, seen for miles around.
I nap and grow feathers; I'm not yet as regal
As my mother and dad. I'm a baby Bald Eagle.

Where do I sleep? In a soft, grass-lined nest,
Where tender spring boughs hide the place that I rest.
My mother sings sweetly and tells me to hush
At dusk and at dawn. I'm a wee Hermit Thrush.

Where do I sleep? Underneath the low trees,
Close to my mother, my head on my knees.
Someday I'll be grown and my spots will be gone.
I dream of that now; I'm a Blacktail Deer fawn.

Where do I sleep? In a cave dark and deep,
Where all of us hang upside down by our feet.
My home is as black as a Halloween cat.
I fly in the night; I'm a young Brown Bat.

Where do I sleep? On the high mountainside—
Way out in the open, I see far and wide.
With little black hooves and a snowy fur coat,
I'm sure of my feet. I'm a young Mountain Goat.

Where do I sleep? In a well-hidden place,
Wearing rings on my tail and spots on my face.
Someday I will roam in a wilderness lit
By the bright moon and stars. I'm a young Cougar kit.

Where do I sleep? Between far northern lakes,
Where thickets of willow act as windbreaks.
Rambling the forest, my legs long and loose,
I'll grow up to be a magnificent Moose.

Where do I sleep? You can hear my sharp call
From a mossy nest behind a waterfall.
Where the rocks are worn smooth as an old satin slipper,
And the soft mist is cool—I'm a young Water Dipper.

Where do I sleep? In a cool, shaded stream
That shimmers like silver as I drift and dream.
Swimming downstream to the sea by and by,
I'll return when I'm grown. I'm a Salmon fry.

Where do I sleep? In a den underground,
Lined with velvety grass—it's here I'll be found.
In a russet red coat with sooty black socks
And bright golden eyes, I'm a baby Red Fox.

Where do I sleep? In a web that I wove
Of glistening threads—it's a real treasure trove.
When dewdrops sparkle and day becomes lighter
Look close and you'll see: I'm a Garden Spider.

Where do I sleep? In a bunk bed down low.
The top bunk is where my stuffed animals go.
I have my own blanket and teddy bear, too.
I'm a little human child, just like you.

For my mother and father, who read to me
And took us all to the library;
And when I could read for myself instead,
They placed a light at the head of my bed.
And they'd come in to check at dawn
To find my little lamp still on.
Some things don't change that much, they say
My reading light's still on today.

With special thanks to Sara, David, Marion, Lorraine,
Uncle Bobby, Mr. Woodwick, and Miss Molly Jane.
—J. B.

This work is dedicatd to my family with immense
gratitude for their love, faith, and unfaltering support. Thank you!
—A. G.

Text copyright ©2001 by Jennifer Blomgren
Illustrations copyright ©2001 by Andrea Gabriel

Cover and interior design: Karen Schober
Printed in China

Distributed by Publishers Group West
07 06 05   5

Library of Congress Cataloging in Publication Data
Blomgren, Jennifer.
Where do I sleep? : a Pacific Northwest lullaby / Jennifer Blomgren ; illustrated by Andrea Gabriel.
p. cm.
Summary: Rhyming text describes young animals—from a gray wolf pup and a horned puffin
to a cougar kit and a small brown bat—as they settle down to sleep.
ISBN 1-57061-258-7
[1. Animals—Infancy—Fiction. 2. Sleep—Fiction. 3. Lullabies.
4. Stories in rhyme.] I. Gabriel, Andrea, ill. II. Title.

PZ8.3.B59833 Wh 2001
[E]—dc21   2001020940

Sasquatch Books
119 South Main Street, Suite 400
Seattle, Washington 98104
(206) 467-4300
www.SasquatchBooks.com
custserv@sasquatchbooks.com